FREDDIE

FLOSSIE

The BOBBSEY TWINS®

THE MYSTERY OF THE GHOST IN THE ATTIC

By Laura Lee Hope

Illustrated by Larry Ruppert

Little Simon

New York London Toronto Sydney

NAN

BERT

LITTLE SIMON

An imprint of Simon & Schuster Children's Publishing Division

1230 Avenue of the Americas, New York, New York 10020

Copyright © 2005 by Simon & Schuster, Inc.

All rights reserved, including the right of reproduction in whole or in part in any form.

LITTLE SIMON is a registered trademark of Simon & Schuster, Inc., and associated

colophon is a trademark of Simon & Schuster, Inc.

Produced by Cheshire Studio

Manufactured in the United States of America

First Edition

2 4 6 8 10 9 7 5 3 1

ISBN-13: 978-1-4169-0704-6

ISBN-10: 1-4169-0704-1

"Mom, Mom, there's a ghost in the house!" exclaimed Freddie Bobbsey as he and his sister Flossie ran down the stairs one morning.

"There's no such thing as ghosts," said Mrs. Bobbsey as the twins burst into the kitchen. She had just baked delicious-smelling cookies and was now starting on breakfast.

"But we heard strange scratching noises last night!" said Flossie.

"And a big crash!" said Freddie.

"Your father and I didn't hear anything," said their mother gently. "Did you see any ghosts when you were playing in the attic yesterday?"

"No, but ghosts don't come out in the daytime," said Freddie. "Can we go up to the attic and investigate?"

"No. Go up to your *room* and get dressed. You can investigate after school," Mrs. Bobbsey said.

Freddie and Flossie thought the school day would *never* end. When they finally got home, they headed up to the attic with a plate of cookies.

"Look," said Flossie, pointing to a pile of blocks. It had been a castle the day before.

"That must have been the big crash we heard!" said Freddie.

"So it *wasn't* a dream!" said Flossie. "But why did the castle tip over? Someone—or *something*—must have knocked it down!"

Freddie looked out the window. "No one could have climbed up here," he said, "and the window is too small to get through anyway. It must have been a ghost!"

Freddie and Flossie rebuilt the castle.

"I wish Nan and Bert were here," said Flossie. "They're both so good at solving mysteries."

Nan and Bert were the older Bobbsey twins. They were in nearby Sanderville on a school trip and wouldn't be back until the next morning.

When it was time to set the dinner table the twins turned off the light and started down the stairs.

"Well," said Flossie as she closed the trapdoor, "I guess we'll have to solve this mystery by ourselves."

When they heard a car pull in to the driveway, Freddie and Flossie went outside to greet their father.

"Daddy!" they cried as they ran into his arms. "There's a ghost in the attic! A *real* ghost!"

As the Bobbseys ate dinner the twins told their Dad all about the noises they had heard the night before and the wrecked castle in the attic.

"No one could have climbed into the attic through the window," said Freddie. "It must have been a ghost. What else could have knocked over the castle?"

"That's a real mystery," said Mr. Bobbsey.
"Whatever it was, Freddie," said Mrs. Bobbsey,
"it *wasn't* a ghost."

When it was time for bed Mr. Bobbsey gave Freddie a flashlight in case he and Flossie got scared.

"Don't worry," said Mrs. Bobbsey as she kissed Flossie good night. "If you hear anything, just come down the hall and wake us up."

After their parents left, the twins lay awake listening for strange noises. But it had been such an exciting day, they soon fell asleep, until . . .

Crash! They were awakened by a loud noise coming from the attic!

This time Mr. and Mrs. Bobbsey heard the mysterious sound too.

"Maybe you should let me go up there," Mr. Bobbsey said as he started down the hall. But it was too late. Freddie and Flossie were already lifting the trapdoor.

As Freddie shined his flashlight into the darkness, he whispered, "What's that m-m-moving over by the castle?"

"It's a squirrel—and he's eating one of mom's cookies!" Flossie said, laughing.

"What's he doing up here?" asked Freddie. "Where's the ghost?"

Mr. Bobbsey rushed in after the twins, grabbing a fishing net, and Freddie helped him catch the squirrel. Flossie helped him stick the net out the window to free the squirrel onto the roof.

"Now let's look for the ghost," said Freddie.
"But there *is* no ghost," said Flossie.
Freddie looked puzzled. "What do you mean?"

"When we left the attic window open the other day, the squirrel came inside," Flossie said with a smile. "*He's* the one who made the scratching noises and knocked over the castle."

"Congratulations!" said Mr. Bobbsey. "It looks like you two have solved the mystery of the ghost in the attic."